Floppy and the Bone

Written by Cynthia Rider
based on the original characters
created by Roderick Hunt and Alex Brychta
Illustrated by Alex Brychta

OXFORD
UNIVERSITY PRESS

Floppy saw a big bone.

"I want that bone,"
said Floppy.

He got the bone!

"Stop! Stop!" said Biff.

"Drop the bone!" said Chip.

But Floppy did not stop,
and he did not drop the bone!

He ran up the hill.

He ran into a wood…

and onto a bridge…
and he stopped!

Floppy looked down.

He saw a dog in the water.

The dog had a big bone.

Floppy wanted that bone, too.

Grrrrrrrrr!

went Floppy.

SPLASH! went the bone.
SPLASH! went Floppy.

"Oh no!" said Floppy.
"The dog I saw was me!"

Talk about the story

Why do you think Floppy took the bone?

What did Floppy see in the water? Did he think it was a real dog?

Do you think Floppy was a sensible dog in this story?

Have you ever wanted something as much as Floppy wanted his bone?

Picture puzzle

How many things can you find beginning with the same sound as the 'b' in ball?

(Answer to picture puzzle: ball, bike, bottle, bowl, boy, bush, butterfly)